Ellie marches on

by Audra Notgrass

For Henry, Toby, and Sloan

yipjar Book Design by yipjar.com

STORYBOOK GENIUS PUBLISHING
sbgpublishing.com

The winter I was five was a cold one.
It rained, but the rain never turned to snow.

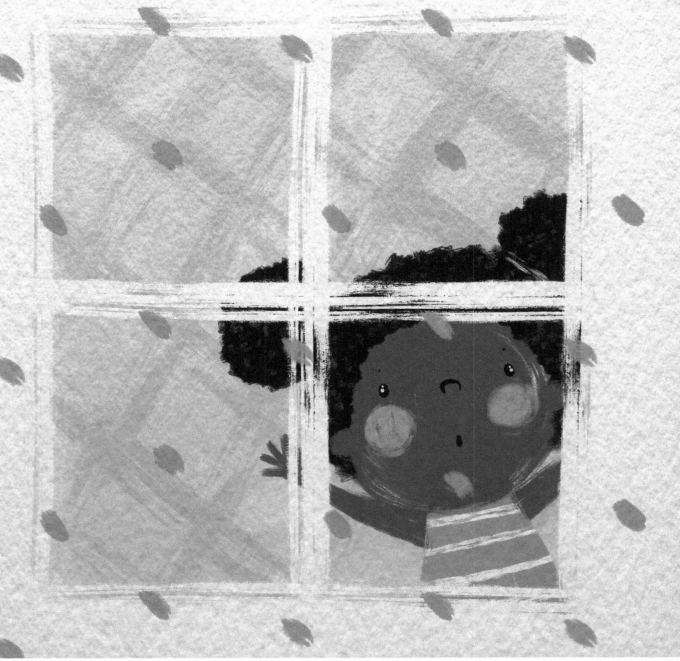

I went to school,
played video games,
and hung out with
my best friend, Nafia.

Nafia didn't have many friends.
She was new to the neighborhood
and didn't speak much English.

Once while we were eating lunch, Parker came over
to our table. He started calling Nafia mean names
and took away her food.

"Stop that!" I cried.
But Parker kept on calling her names and
shouting at her to go home.
I jumped up, grabbed
Nafia's food and yelled
at Parker to go away.

Seeing Nafia hurt by
mean kids made me sad.
It didn't matter that
we were different.
She was my best
friend and I was hers.

One night, I was in the kitchen getting a snack.

Mama and her friend, Ash, were bent over large foam boards. Paint was everywhere and music played in the background.

I wandered over to the table and Mama looked up.
"Whatcha doin?" I asked as Mama and Ash stopped their work.

"Well," Mama said slowly. "A lot of people think Nafia
shouldn't live here. They think she should go back to
the country where she was born. Those people are being
very unkind. Their kids hear their parents talking at home
and they repeat what they hear at school. It hurts Nafia
very much. Do you remember how the kids at school treat
Nafia?" Mama asked.

I nodded.

"But Mama, that's not right! And it's not fair!
I like her living here. I don't want her to move away!"

"No, it's not right. But we can help. We can let people
know that we will work hard to protect Nafia."

Then Mama and Ash told me about some brave women who stood up for what is right.

They told me about Alice Walker, a writer who speaks out for human rights.

They told me about Hillary Clinton,

a politician who has spent her life working
for the fair treatment of others.

And they told me about Coretta Scott King, an activist who fought her whole life for civil rights and racial justice.

"There are many women who worked tirelessly so that girls like Nafia and you could make your own choices, go to school, and be themselves. Sometimes people were mean to these brave women. But they fought hard to earn and protect the rights of all girls. They never gave up, even when they wanted to," Mama said.

"Mama, how can I help like these women did?"

"Tomorrow, Ash and I are going to the city to march with hundreds of people. We are going to show people that we care about Nafia and that we are willing to work hard to make our country safe and free for everyone. You are welcome to come march with us," Mama said.

"I'm going to come with you, and I'm going to make a sign!
Mama! Can Nafia come with me?" I asked.

"Yes she can,
if her parents say it's OK."

I was so excited that I jumped to my feet and ran all the way to Nafia's house. I told Nafia all about the march and she wanted to come with me. Her mom said it was OK!

We worked very hard on our signs.
They had to be the most beautiful
signs we could make.

The very next
morning we went
to the march!
It was packed.
It was colorful.
The sun was
shining and it
was beautiful.

I clutched my sign as we began to walk. I remembered the stories about Alice, Hillary and Coretta. I remembered the struggles and the victories. I thought about the hard work they did, so I could march today. My heart swelled with gratefulness.

The long line of women marching
stretched out in front of me.
And behind me the line was so long,
I imagined it fading into the past.

Gripping my sign tighter, I turned my
face toward the sun. Hand in hand
with my best friend Nafia,
we marched on.

CPSIA information can be obtained
at www.ICGtesting.com
Printed in the USA
LVHW070737080620
657647LV00031B/329